A Chinese Folktale

Mei Ming
and the
Dragon's
Daughter

Retold by   Illustrated by

Lydia Bailey  Martin Springett

Scholastic Canada Ltd.

Scholastic Canada Ltd.
123 Newkirk Road, Richmond Hill, Ontario, Canada L4C 3G5

Scholastic Inc.
730 Broadway, New York, NY 10003, USA

Ashton Scholastic Pty Limited
PO Box 579, Gosford, NSW 2250, Australia

Ashton Scholastic Limited
Private Bag 1, Penrose, Auckland, New Zealand

Scholastic Publications Ltd.
Villiers House, Clarendon Avenue, Leamington Spa,
Warwickshire CV32 5PR, UK

Canadian Cataloguing in Publication Data

Bailey, Lydia
  Mei Ming and the dragon's daughter

ISBN 0-590-73370-2

I. Springett, Martin. II. Title.

PS8553.A55M4 1991   jC813'.54   C90-094080-8
PZ7.B3Me 1991

6 5 4 3 2 1   Printed in Hong Kong   2 3 4 5/9

ONCE UPON A DRAGON'S TALE

there lived a young girl who had a singing voice as sweet as a nightingale's. The girl, Mei Ming, lived with her father in a tiny hut at the foot of a great mountain.

Every morning Mei Ming rose before dawn, prepared her father a pot of rice, and went into the fields to cut bamboo. Every evening she sat in front of the fire weaving the long bamboo reeds into brooms for her father to sell in the marketplace. As she worked, she sang in a clear and gentle voice:

Fish have fins and birds have wings.
I've one small voice
But I can sing.

And every night she would sing her father to sleep with lullabies of rushing rivers and wondrous waterfalls.

For many months there was no rain in Mei Ming's village. The rice turned brown, the tall green stalks of bamboo yellowed and died, and the stream bed dried into an empty, ugly scar running through the village. The people of the village hung their heads in sadness. And still there was no rain.

The land became drier and drier and Mei Ming had to walk farther and farther to find even a few withered stalks of bamboo.

One hot day, having found not even the tiniest green shoot in the valley, she decided to search on the mountain. Ever higher she climbed, until she was walking among the clouds. For the first time in many days Mei Ming forgot her thirst.

When at last she reached the top, she gasped with surprise. There, nestled in a thicket of fresh bamboo, was a beautiful blue lake. This will be my secret lake, she thought delightedly. She knelt to drink its cool waters, then filled her arms with the green bamboo and returned home.

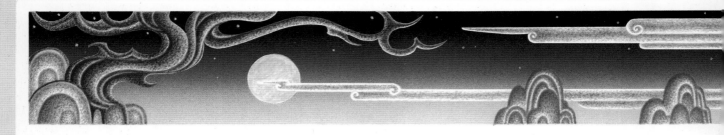

That night Mei Ming had disturbing dreams. She saw the beautiful blue lake suspended above her village and all the people reaching up to it with their empty water buckets. And she knew she could not keep her lake a secret.

She rose early the next morning. She had a plan. With a small digging shovel on her back and a smile on her face, she carefully followed the path back up to the top of the mountain. There, as blue and peaceful as the day before, lay the sparkling lake. If I can dig an opening, Mei Ming thought, the waters of the lake will spill down the side of the mountain and the people of my village need never be thirsty again.

But the edge of the lake was surrounded by great stones and before three quarters of an hour had passed, her shovel was bent and broken. In frustration she threw it down and it fell into the water. As she reached for it, she saw a big stone gate shimmering just beneath the surface of the lake.

She tried to pry the gate open with her shovel, but it refused to move and she saw that it was bolted with a huge iron lock. Discouraged, she sat down on a rock and stared at the gate. If I can neither dig a hole nor open the gate, she thought, how can I help the people of my village?

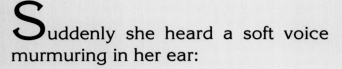

Suddenly she heard a soft voice murmuring in her ear:

If an open gate
*   you wish to see,*
You first must find
*   the golden key.*

Mei Ming looked around in astonishment. The only thing she saw was a wild goose gliding silently and serenely on the lake far out from shore. Was it the goose who spoke to me? she wondered. But just then the bird spread its wings and gracefully arched up over the lake and into the forest.

Mei Ming was puzzled but determined to find the key. She searched the shore of the lake until she came to a grove of cypress trees, where she heard a great squawking and beating of wings. Perched on a gnarled branch high above her head were three birds the color of jewels. Their screeching seemed to say:

> *If you want to free
>   the water,
> You first must seek
>   the dragon's daughter.*

Then they lifted their wings and flapped noisily off into the forest.

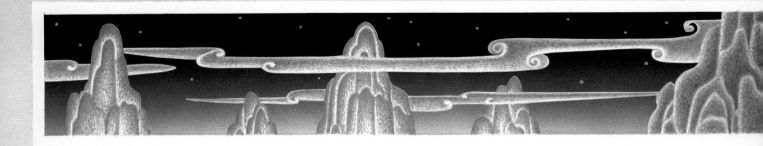

Who is the dragon, Mei Ming wondered, and where can I find his daughter?

No sooner had the question occurred to her than she saw a peacock standing lone and haughty before her on the path. Shaking its tail into a great blue-green fan, it turned and strutted silently into the forest. But as it disappeared, she heard a soft cooing in her ears:

> *The dragon's daughter charmed will be,*
> *And come at your request,*
> *If beside the lake you sing*
> *The songs you love the best.*

Mei Ming thought for a moment and sang back her reply:

> *Fish have fins and birds have wings.*
> *I've one small voice —*
> *Yes, I can sing.*

Then, in a voice strong and clear, she sang of white horses galloping in glistening fields of snow. She sang of lotus blossoms floating on lakes. And she sang of mountain tops wreathed in mists.

But the dragon's daughter did not come.

If beautiful songs won't call her, thought Mei Ming, perhaps brave ones will.

In a stronger voice she began to sing songs of her village in the valley. She sang of farmers who tried to grow rice in fields that were bone dry. She sang of mothers, endlessly weaving their baskets and brooms to barter for food for their children.

And still the dragon's daughter did not come.

Tears began to stream down Mei Ming's face as she sang of her beloved father and how hard his life had become.

Suddenly, with a flip of her tail, the dragon's daughter appeared, her long hair streaming behind her in the water. "Who are you," she inquired kindly, "and why do you sing such sad and beautiful songs?"

"My name is Mei Ming and I need the key to open the gate," she pleaded. "Without the waters from the lake, the people of my village will surely die."

"My father is guarding the key in his cave at the bottom of the lake, and he will surely eat you if you try to take it," the dragon's daughter replied. "But I cannot bear to see you weep. Come, let us sing together of happy things, and perhaps our songs will put him to sleep. Then you could swim past him into the cave and look for the key."

And so Mei Ming and the dragon's daughter joined their voices in song. They sang shyly, they sang softly:

> *The sun is sparkling on the waves,*
> *The air is warm and sweet.*
> *So why then hide yourself away*
> *In sorrowful retreat?*

They sang sweetly, they sang pleadingly:

> *To view the wonders of the world,*
> *A wanderer you must be.*
> *And if you live a thousand years*
> *You'll still find more to see.*

Far beneath the lake they could hear the old dragon snorting and roaring. But as they continued to sing their sweet songs, he got quieter and quieter. Before long, there was silence in the cave below. "Go now," said the dragon's daughter, gently tugging on Mei Ming's arm.

Into the lake she dove, swimming deeper and deeper, down through the icy waters to the very bottom. The dragon lay sprawled at the cave's entrance, one red eye open, one eye closed. Mei Ming slid silently past him into the cave, taking care not to brush against his sharp scales.

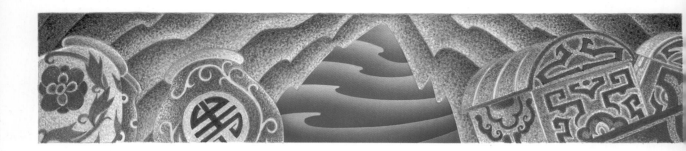

She could not believe the riches that lay before her. There were trunks overflowing with fine embroidered silks. There were golden urns that held diamonds and rubies and lustrous pearls. Mei Ming gazed around her in wonderment, longing to fill her pockets with the dragon's jewels. But what help are jewels to thirsty people? she thought, and she continued her search for the key.

She searched everywhere, without luck. Then, just as she was losing hope, she accidentally knocked against a small ebony box and a large golden key fell to the ground. Closing her fingers around it, Mei Ming swam quickly out of the cave, past the sleeping dragon, to the shore above.

With shaking hands she inserted the key into the big iron lock. She turned it carefully to the left and carefully to the right. Suddenly she heard a click and the gate opened with a shudder, releasing the clear blue waters of the lake. The water poured down the mountainside in a sparkling waterfall, filling the dry stream in the village below.

With the dragon's daughter swimming at her side, Mei Ming skipped down the side of the mountain, the angry roars of the dragon fading with each step she took. By the time they reached the village, the dry stream had become a mighty rushing river.

From that day on, the dragon's daughter lived in the river where it ran past Mei Ming's small hut. Each morning at sunrise Mei Ming would stand at the river's edge and awaken her with these words:

Fish have fins
and birds have wings.
We've two small voices.
Come out! Let's sing!

They spent their days laughing and teaching each other their favorite songs. And each evening at sunset the people of the village could hear them singing their songs together, their voices joined as one in joy and friendship.